CH00733614

ANCIENT ADVENTURES

ACROSS THE AGES

Edited By Sarah Washer

Years of

First published in Great Britain in 2017 by:

YoungWriters

Coltsfoot Drive
Peterborough
PE2 9BF
Telephone: 01733 890066
Website: www.youngwriters.co.uk

All Rights Reserved
Book Design by Ashley Janson
© Copyright Contributors 2016
SB ISBN 978-1-78624-651-6
Printed and bound in the UK by BookPrintingUK
Website: www.bookprintinguk.com
YB0292T

FOREWORD

Welcome, Reader, to 'Ancient Adventures – Across The Ages'.
Have you ever wondered what it would be like if you stepped back in
time? Well, for Young Writers' latest competition, we asked our
writers nationwide to travel back in time and create a story with a
beginning, middle and end, with the added challenge of using no
more than 100 words.

The result is this collection of fantastic storytelling that covers a whole
host of different topics. You will be transported to all types of different
adventures and, I'm sure, will learn something new with each story
you read. Perhaps you'll enjoy taking a trip to witness war and brutal
battles, dare to discover deadly dinosaurs, come face-to-face with
vicious Vikings, or find yourself getting all wrapped up with the
mummies in ancient Egypt! This collection has a story to suit
everyone.

There was a great response to this competition which is always nice to
see, and the standard of entries was excellent, so I'd like to say a big
thank you and congratulations to everyone who entered for your
amazing adventures.

I hope you enjoy reading these mini sagas as much as I did.

Keep writing!
Sarah Washer

CONTENTS

Georgia Beck (11)	56
Durlav Katwal (11)	57
Nyah Phoenix (11)	58
Adam Ehsan (10)	59
Samuel Hockley (11)	60
Poppy Jones (10)	61
Corey Yuile (11)	62
Eiman Zahid (10)	63
Olivia Rhodes (11)	64
Leo Drew (11)	65

St John The Baptist Primary School, London

Taya Edwards-Sowomi (10)	66
Darren Osei Sarfo (10)	67
Jason O'Connor (10)	68
Royal Edorh (10)	69
Daniel Aduqbole (10)	70
Grace Cole (10)	71
Aalenya Reece (10)	72

St Paul's CE Primary School, London

Cecile Reeves (10)	73
Fope Haroun (9)	74
Lyra Butcher (9)	75
Leon Francis White (9)	76
Ariel Leeb (9)	77
Lucy-Lou Collis (9)	78
Luke Naumovic (9)	79
Aisha Abdulaziz (9)	80
Harvey Nightingale (9)	81
Amelia Pike (9)	82
Aylan Touat (9)	83
Max Scantlebury (9)	84
Saira Ali (9)	85
Felix Pinyol (9)	86
Anine Christinsen (9)	87
Martha Reynolds (9)	88

Dario Velazquez (9)	89
Aadam Muhammad (9)	90
Alice Warden (9)	91

St Peter's Catholic Primary School, Leamington Spa

Júlia Viguier Souto (9)	92
Luke Cashman (8)	93
James Foley (10)	94
Thomas Connell (9)	95
Daniel Bodely (9)	96
Ben Foley (8)	97
Zach Miah (8)	98
Maisie Young (9)	99
Ropa Kazora (8)	100
Oli Passantino (8)	101
Sebastian Bainbridge (9)	102
Jack Dando (9)	103
Loretta Memetovic (9)	104
Wiki Jakubczyk (8)	105
Guilherme Berlino Pinto (8)	106
Samuel Divers (8)	107
Amelia Smith (8)	108
James Pearson (9)	109
Kieran O'Connor (9)	110
Valentin Bonnet-Aumann (8)	111

Thomas's Academy, London

Aaron Rye Bumagat (8)	112
Ricco De Beaufort	113
Rihanna Andrews (8)	114
Basma Djenadou (8)	115
Lewis Baptiste (8)	116
Anum Muktar (8)	117
Kaci Agullo (8)	118
Noah Quicksell (8)	119

Whithorn Primary School, Newton Stewart

Kristian Fisher (9)	120
Ciara Jolly (11)	121
Lexi Fisher (11)	122
Ryan Williams (8)	123
Sean Collins (10)	124
Shiloh Boyce (7)	125
Amy Vance (8)	126

THE MINI SAGAS

The Founding Of Niagara Falls

'Daughter! Your suitor awaits you, my sweet,' Father cried out, just as I was about to walk down the cold, stone steps. I heard several excited whispers from guests.

Father handed me over to a bear of a man, who was said to be an old king. I took off with my coat, running. My real love was the god of thunder, He-No. I jumped into my canoe and paddled into the strong currents. I sailed down the falls! He-No swooped me into his arms, saving me! Ever since, locals and foreigners have been fighting over the peaceful miracle land.

Nidhi Joshi (10)

The Conscience Of Thomas Farriner

In September 1666, at Pudding Lane, a fire developed at Farriner's bakery.

'Thomas, rise. I am your conscience. A spark has fallen on a bundle of sticks. I sense a fire. Do something, this could ruin London.'

He did something: he woke his family, including the maid. There were going to escape by climbing out an upstairs window to the neighbours', all but the maid. She burnt along with the many houses that burnt in the four days of the fire. Thomas continued to hear my vexatious voice; he didn't attempt to do anything about the fire that ruined London.

Abena Asamoah-Djan (11)

The Vikings' Hunt

Thor and Loki built a big boat at Peterhead. They put the weapons on the boat, then they were heading to Cruden Bay.
Eight hours later they arrived at Cruden Bay. Another boat came, slowing down. They tied the boat to a rusty pole. They had a battle with the other Vikings. After the battle they went back to Peterhead. They had many other battles at Peterhead.

Ethan Wilson (9)

The Castle Siege

A bellowing horn echoed around the great hall. An attack had begun! Men ran out, ready to defend as fierce arrows rained down. Ear-splitting screams ran through the infantry as hot lead flew from the castle murder holes. Inside, men fled as angry stone cannonballs flew towards them. Behind the castle and safe from the attackers, a young boy climbed up the secret steps from the sea and delivered much-needed supplies. Knowing Harlech's strength and vital coastal access, King Edward sat proudly on his throne. The terrifying siege of 1294 lasted a whole year, but the castle held strong.

Aimee Dalby (8)

Cleopatra's Missing Emblem

One beautifully sweltering day, just off the coast of Egypt, the most influential, dominant and mightiest queen had a very important dilemma! Cleopatra could not find her prized possession: her emblem, the Eye of Horus. Without this she would not have protection. 'Oh what am I going to do without my beauty?' she sobbed. Turning her home upside down, Cleopatra could not find her emblem anywhere! Eventually she gave up and decided to get ready without it. She sat down in front of her mirror and found that she had been wearing it all throughout the day! Silly Cleopatra!

Darcy-Lula Kearns (11)

The Vikings

At exactly 9 o'clock in the morning, when the whole town was fast asleep, there was a loud creak! Then a thud! Suddenly, Fred woke up. He peeked out of his window and screamed in horror. At this moment the whole town was awake. Outside was a massive wooden boat. 'Vikings!' he shouted. He sprinted downstairs and up to the town museum. He grabbed the most precious thing in the town - the grand sword - and locked it in a titanium safe so no one could get it. Eventually, the Vikings won and took everything valuable except for one thing…

Lucas Crabbe (9)

The Pyramid Thieves

I was really excited, finally we were getting to study the pyramid. It was boiling hot. Mum and I were finally at the door to the pyramid. Oh my gosh, we couldn't believe our eyes; diamonds, silver, gold and jewels were still inside the pyramid's tomb. Incredible! How much might this treasure be worth and how much could we steal? I quickly checked my pockets and emptied my backpack. Stealthily, we began to fill our bag with treasure. We crammed as much as we could and began to plan our escape. Suddenly, the security guard looked up...

Gerry Forrest (7)

Hunting

In the morning, Nono woke up in the freezing cold cave. Nono went over to Charchar's bed and gave him a little nudge, but he was out cold. He went outside but immediately Nono felt like an ice cube, so quickly went back inside. Nono was surprised to see that Charchar was awake. They started to get some tools. They went out and travelled far and wide and saw a massive deer. Charchar got his spear and threw it and it hit the deer. 'Yay!' They finally had something good to eat other than disgusting nuts and berries.

Noah Mitchell (8)

Spartan School

It was a bright morning when Nero woke up. He rushed downstairs to eat. Then went through to the door to Spartan school where he met his best friend Markus. Nero and Markus realised they were late so they ran to spear practice class. When they got there Mr Grumpicus shouted at them then handed everyone a spear. He told Nero to throw the spear at a target. First he threw it and it missed, then he aimed, threw it and hit the target. The whole class cheered and he felt proud. He knew he would be a great warrior.

Zara Ahmad (8)

Quick Shutdown

Staggering into the room, memories fill me, tearing me apart like a dagger piercing through my soul. I know what I have done and the weight of the burden drags me down. Scenes flash before my eyes, horrific scenes. My head burns with fury. Suddenly, out of the corner of my eye, glistening in the light, is my black gun. I gently hold it up and rest it on the side of my head. All it would take is one shot, one trigger, one bullet. My finger slowly presses the handle. I am Adolf Hitler and I changed the world.

Samantha Dias (11)

The Kidnapper

There were two girls called Freya and Lucy. They were homeless. They found a shed in the forest to sleep in. When they got there, they saw a dog and they called him Jacob. That night they saw a face. Jacob started barking. They woke up and stayed still. They saw a face again. The face took them into an old barn. For their breakfast they had a glass of milk. When he went they found a key. They tried to open the door. It opened and they rushed to the telephone. They rang the police who took him.

Tabitha Smith (9)

The Ghost Of King Henry VIII

Long ago, I was working all alone when I saw a flicker ahead of me. I tried to convince myself that it was a strong wind... I carried on working harder than before. Suddenly, without warning, a face came out of the tower door (or should I say through it?) he had a bearded chin, an evil smile... yellow teeth. He seemed to be wanting me to follow him into the dark forest a little way ahead. I then noticed he had no legs and was floating in mid-air. It was the ghost of King Henry VIII...

Mina Stojkovic (10)

Egypt

Once, there was a bird. The bird's name was Brussle. He went on an adventure. He was so excited, but there was a bird hunter! Brussle took him out by grabbing his crossbow. He missed. Brussle hit him on the head. He was unconscious for, I guess, five minutes. He found an Egyptian tomb and a gravestone. He was frightened like hell, so he ran and ran until he was out of sight. Suddenly, someone got him somehow. I couldn't believe it; it was impossible. How? Why? Somehow.

Joshuah Wheeler (7)

The Worst Mummy Ever!

The mummy was the worst mummy ever and he found Khufu and he stole his bandages! He chopped him up and he stabbed him with a knife. He locked him up forever. He managed to get out of the coffin and he got out and started to fight the mummy and then he lost. But then another mummy came out of the walls and triggered a trap, and the whole entire pyramid came down because of a big earthquake! Then he ran away and the mummy chased after him and he ran away forever.

Ryan Dawson (7)

The Big Storm

It was a dark night. There was a little girl called Louise and she was with her parents. One night, the army knocked at every house telling them every child must be evacuated to the countryside. Louise was on a train the next day but there was a big storm. Everything went off. They had to sleep on the train. There was a thunderous noise. Suddenly, the train was working and they all made it to Wales' countryside safely.

Imogen Bell (10)

The Magic Temple

One day, I went on an ancient adventure. I started off walking in the centre of an enormous building. I went to investigate inside. When I went in, it was very big and very black. Then, suddenly, out of the corner of my eye I saw a big shiny cave. In the cave I saw a lot of guards walking around. I then found one of my friends called Janice. We went in the cave together and we found a lot of gold. We then started to head off. We got home and then we laughed.

Isabella Conreno (9)
All Saints' Primary School, Airdrie

The Great Escape!

I shivered as I walked through the gloomy wood. Who knew if someone would jump out and rip me to smithereens and cook me for dinner? Corner to corner I looked. *Bang!* 'Oow, help me!'
All of a sudden, a nurse appeared and said, 'Hello, my name is Florence Nightingale and I am here to help you.'
'OK,' I stammered, 'but first, where am I?' I asked.
'On the battlefield darling, in the battlefield, but just come with me.'
'I can't.'
'Why not?'
'I can't walk.'
'OK, just let me pick you up and bring you to a bed.'

Eve Robinson (9)
Eaton Primary School, Tarporley

Greek Gods

'Where am I?' I asked, wondering.

'My friend, you're in ancient Greece, the land of wonder. I'm the almighty Zeus, the god of thunder!' he shouted. Then it clicked; these were the Greek gods of old, Hera, Zeus and Athena, three gods from ancient Greece. I started to approach Athena who was looking at her owls.

'Hello Athena,' I murmured.

'How may I help you?' Athena replied.

'Please tell me why I'm here,' I asked.

'You were brought here for good reasons, I can't tell you, you must find out for yourself… '

Charley Gittins (10)
Eaton Primary School, Tarporley

The Romans In The Past...

'It's 21:45 on 11th February 48 AD, and I'm in the dirty, gloomy, pitch-black Roman Colosseum! At 22:35 the midnight fight - which isn't actually at midnight - will begin!'
Five minutes later…
The emperor called out as loudly as he could when they were milliseconds away from fighting, 'Let the battle commence!'
My heart froze. It was pounding faster than a speed record. My eyes welled up with enormous, crystal-clear tears; I then looked up again and I noticed there was a hole in the fighter's leg. I really hoped that the petrifying fight would finish as soon as possible…

Henry Page (9)
Eaton Primary School, Tarporley

The Romans Against The Latins: Total War!

In the year 72 AD, the Romans (with the look of anger and rage on their faces) were only minutes away from an unmissable life-risking battle against the Latins. Then, the battle commenced. 'Attack!' shouted the Roman leader.

'Impetus!' bellowed the Latin. Everyone started to run onto the battlefield in groups of 30-50. Both the clans had the equal amount of battle skill, the war went on for a long time.

Eventually, the Romans won with only a group of 16 left, and found out that the Latins only attacked to rule their villages and country.

Ethan Davies (9)
Eaton Primary School, Tarporley

Henry And The Mummy

One boiling hot day in the middle of ancient Egypt, Henry VIII was digging for shiny, golden, legendary treasure. He stumbled across an enormous hole. Suddenly, he fell in, shouting, 'Help!' He saw a wrapped, rotten mummy thing. It turned to midnight sky. Smoke puffed in anger. Green rot and slime oozed out of his bony body. He had foul breath, it smelt of mouldy cheese and rotten eggs. He yelled, 'Who dares disturb my sleep?'
'Henry VIII, you're a slimy drop of a crocodile's breath.'
'What!'

Joseph Plant (8)
Eaton Primary School, Tarporley

Off We Go Down The Street

One day, Bruce and I were playing hopscotch when a tiger came towards us and *roared!* So before it attacked, I slayed it. A little later, my dad, came by and said, 'We're going to the water park.'
When we arrived at the water park I went down the slide what felt like *10,000 times!* Bruce was busy diving, then after a long day we went to bed.
In the morning, Dad drew pictures on the wall, we saw what he did, so we drew *more and more!* Then we decided to played tag for the rest of the day.

Alexander Newton (7)
Eaton Primary School, Tarporley

The Roman's News

'Charge!' King Home yelled. 'Slay the lions!' The Roman soldiers got their spears out and killed the lion.

Meanwhile, Bruce and Alexander were having lunch until a Roman broke in and snatched Bruce! Bruce was trapped inside an iron cage! Alexander was hiding under a table. *Snap!* The weak table broke and snapped to pieces. The deadly Roman was standing there. What could Bruce do?

Bruce Clarke (7)
Eaton Primary School, Tarporley

They're Coming

The wind was howling like an angry wolf. Sofia and I were sweating so badly as it came. My jaw dropped, my heart was pounding as fast as a car going sixty miles per hour. We started running and running. In a blink of an eye the beast vanished… 'W… w… where is… it? Is it gone?' Sofia whispered, fearing that she would be devoured. 'There!' I replied. I felt so scared. I started to sprint faster until it gulped its prey - me! I bit my tongue, holding my breath. We came face-to-face with the big, bold… dinosaur!

Issy Hool (9)
Eaton Primary School, Tarporley

The Secret Of History

Long, long ago, before the Stone Age, there lived Tutankhamun with Egypt in the palm of his hands. Six years later, in the sudden death of Egypt there was a boy called Peter and his father Andrew. Long before Peter, lived his grandfather, the explorer, who Peter strived to be like. In a blink of an eye a sandstorm blew in and captured Peter's father. 'Will I ever see him again?' Then, from a distance, Peter heard footsteps. *Bang!* The ground was taken from beneath his feet. Then, Peter was gone… Now the rest is history.

Freya Howarth (9)
Eaton Primary School, Tarporley

Henry VIII

I was thinking of my wife, Anne Boleyn, she'd lost another baby. Sadly, it was a boy. I was still thinking of a name. I was feeling like I should get rid of her. I had a brainwave! It was time to get her executed! I told her to follow me, like nothing was happening. She said, 'Why are you taking me to the execution room?'
I shouted, 'Kneel down.' The last I saw of her was in a pool of blood. I walked out of the room. My eye suddenly drew to Jane Seymour, I quietly whistled. 'Whit whoo!'…

Blake Snary (10)
Eaton Primary School, Tarporley

World War Surprise

One early morning, Callum was walking back from the shops with some out-of-date milk for his early morning hot chocolate. All of a sudden, a huge, scary, massive tornado hit the young, innocent, really dumb Callum. He was screaming, 'Argh!' Then Callum was in, well… he didn't really actually know where he was.

A sergeant major came and said, 'Get your outfit on now, you are not at home.' Callum got given a gun and fought with all the other soldiers. Then he got shot…

Sophie Jane Bowes (9)
Eaton Primary School, Tarporley

The History Of Cavemen

Hi, my name is Jamie and this is my story.
One sunny morning, I was hot and sweaty so I decided to ask my dad if I could play outside. He replied, 'Sure son,' so I did. When I was playing outside, I discovered a deep, dark tunnel. When I went through I found disgusting, fat cavemen. What should I do? Maybe I should explore. I found golden, shiny treasure so I got some of it. When I got the treasure the cavemen were back. They were after me. 'What should I do? Help me please.'

Jamie Willacey (8)
Eaton Primary School, Tarporley

Greece

It was a dark, gloomy Friday night when I was on the boat to Greece with my siblings, Jack, Martha and Thomas. With me being the oldest, it was my duty to look after my siblings. The reason we were going to Greece was because of the war. We were looking for our parents. Suddenly, the boat stopped and the captain announced that we had reached the port. We got our bags and were on the search for our parents.

Years passed and we never found our parents. I was finally giving up hope…

Daisy Plumbley (11)
Eaton Primary School, Tarporley

James Clarke

I was on my way to collect my Victoria Cross from the Queen. I was walking to London from Rochdale, but I had nowhere to sleep, I lay down under a bridge and fell asleep.

In the morning I found myself in a jail cell. I was taken to court, but when the judge found out who I was I was free and the man who arrested me was relieved of his job. I saw the Queen and got my award. My wife and kids were happy for me and even the man who arrested me was there!

Ruben James Clarke (11)
Eaton Primary School, Tarporley

The Frights In The Dark Night

The wind howled, bushes shook. I gasped with fear, 'Who's there? Where am I?'
The sky was as black as a bat. I got up, shaking with fear. Then I heard a grumble. I thought it was my imagination until now as it got louder and louder, then stomping started like the grumble, it got louder and louder. Then, as it got closer I couldn't bear it any more! My heart skipped a beat. At that very moment I was face-to-face with it…

Amelie Mckerrigan (8)
Eaton Primary School, Tarporley

The Monster

The wind was howling and the windows were squeaking open and shut. The door was opening and swiftly moving. I was in the middle of sleeping, it woke me up and gave me a big jump. Have you ever had a jump before?
I went outside, I hid behind a soft, large and furry leaf. I looked behind me then I moved to the other bush. There were insects climbing up the tree. I stretched my arm out to pat the thing and it was a lonely dinosaur!

Holly Quick (7)
Eaton Primary School, Tarporley

The Unknown Vs Romans

History is a great story so why not listen to this story? *Bang!* The Romans roamed through Britain so a little boy, whose place was in a hut in Britain, ran through the chaotic, small village.

Two hours later, he found his way out but now he had to be far away from his home. He definitely knew a place, the abandoned beach, it would be a great place to hide!

Matthew Lee-Emery (9)
Eaton Primary School, Tarporley

War Hog

'Take cover!' my sergeant exclaimed as we caught our breath whilst checking our ammunition. The enemy spoke to each other and kept firing. Suddenly, all of the area was silent. We quietly moved away and vaulted over the stone wall. *Boom!* The sand in front of us exploded like a grenade would. We sprang into action and shot in the opposite direction. Bullets sped past me, one just missed my leg. Suddenly, my waist started to bleed, the stain spread on my tan tactical vest… An attack chopper pulled up in front of us. The gunfire stopped… Everything went silent…

Edward Spence (11)
Eaton Primary School, Tarporley

The Battle Of Waterloo

The clicks of reloading and firing rang in the ears of the French as the battle commenced. A squirt of blood sprayed Wellington: the now one-legged Henry Paget collapsed to the floor. He yelled in pain and suddenly fell silent. His shouting stopped whilst his motionless body was dragged away. The war resumed as the British drove the French back towards the border. Suddenly, the French army broke away: not a French man in sight. Eventually, the firing broke out again. The whole French army were on the Brits; but Napoleon was nowhere in sight. He must have surrendered…

Thomas Kay (10)
Eaton Primary School, Tarporley

The Mummy...

A terrifying monster was hurriedly walking towards me, I was panicking. My dog was behind me, being frightened. The mummy (with shadowy eyes) got closer, he started to look like he was trying to eat me, my heart froze. My dog was barking with a high-sounding voice, I saw blood dripping down his mouth. Immediately, my dog started running, I hid behind the tree. I saw four mummies walking towards me. I quickly ran; however, there was nowhere to run. The mummy eventually surrounded me. As the mummy got closer, my heart started beating faster and faster…

Haruto Greenland (10)
Eaton Primary School, Tarporley

World War Two

September 1st 1939 - September 2nd 1945 - World
War Two… *Bang!* went the Great British bombing.
The screeching, amazingly loud alarm went off.
'Louise, wake up!' said her father. He grabbed
Louise and his wife. They ran as fast as they could,
leaving her brother behind. They ran to the bunker
where they could be counted. Suddenly, there was
a scream, 'Argh! We left Jack behind.' As the wife
climbed out of the bunker to look for him, the father
climbed out as well. Then Louise's mum and dad
were never to be seen again…

Jack Wheeler (8)
Eaton Primary School, Tarporley

Kai The Explorer

One sunny, dry day, way back in ancient history, there was an explorer called Kai. He was famous for his discoveries. One day, he was sent out on a mission to the Valley of the Kings… Just then, Kai slipped and tumbled… *Bang,* went his head. He was trapped in a dark, damp tomb. Kai found a light and went down a corridor congested with sarcophaguses. He came to a stop, opened the door and… found a beast! Tiptoeing behind it, he smashed a pot. *Clang!* It woke the beast. 'Argh!' *Gulp!* Kai was no longer alive.

Joshua John Quick (9)
Eaton Primary School, Tarporley

The War Of History

On one dark, gloomy day during World War II, a little, terrified boy was hiding in an old, run-down shed. *Bang! Bang!* 'Argh, what's that?' the boy shouted. Suddenly, his hands clutched to his feet. The door swung open… leaving a shadow of a mysterious figure. He got swiped off his feet, dragged through the door then *bang!* The door closed. The strange kidnapper took him to a battered, rusty dump. He chucked him into a small car. 'Ouch!' he whispered. He got an electric shock. He crawled out. It was history.

Hettie Sparks (9)
Eaton Primary School, Tarporley

The Exciting Adventure

Bang! Me, a little girl, screamed in fear. My shocked friends and I ran until we were out of breath. Suddenly, we stopped. We found ourselves in a dark wood. It was quiet, almost too quiet… We waited and waited until me and my friends, Martha, Izzy and Amelie, saw *it,* the thing. It had dark eyes and sharp claws. I was scared. I didn't know what it was. It was enormous. It led us into a cave. We went in and noticed it was full of booby traps. We luckily missed them, they all shot something. What was it?

Sofia Vitoria Harvey (8)
Eaton Primary School, Tarporley

World War - A Football Match

Christmas 1914 was the hardest day for soldiers. Instead of being depressed, Henry decided to climb up the ladder. As he went, his fellow soldiers were calling him, but he blocked them out. Once he was out of the trench, he put his arms above his head so the Germans knew he was coming in peace. As Henry walked over to the trench, Achim climbed out. They shook hands; but he didn't say anything. Then every soldier came out of the trenches and played football, but as soon as they came out they were going back again, starting war again.

Suzannah Freeman (11)
Eaton Primary School, Tarporley

Blackbeard

It was November 22nd; I was cornered by two navy troops in dark blue suits at the old and wrinkly side of Queen Anne's revenge; I was terrified. It was really hard taking this big risk, fighting these two brutal captains and their brave crew; it was now or never. I lashed out my sword like a sabre-toothed tiger roaring and shouted, 'All hands on deck!' Unfortunately, some of my crew were on shore which made it even harder; it was almost impossible. As we fought at sea, the vicious waves came onboard, making us all wet!

Calvin Chadwick (10)
Eaton Primary School, Tarporley

Fighting Up The Storm

The storm raged on in the Atlantic Ocean as Sir Francis Drake battled with Black Bart's crew. He was fighting them off when he saw him - Black Bart. He stood at six foot seven, a tall, imposing figure with menacing eyes. They clashed; everything else was blocked out as they fought each other to the death. Sir Francis Drake was backed into a wall but still managed two fatal blows on Bart. He was defeated. Black Bart's crew retreated to their sinking ship, only to go down with it and its treasure. It lies there to this day.

Benjamin Hool (11)
Eaton Primary School, Tarporley

Anne Frank Adventure

Another explosion, I was terrified of the open world. No one but a few, knew this secret my family was holding. This secret was a matter of life and death. Weeks passed and the chance of hunting for Jews was decreasing slowly. The war was coming to an end, but it was still too risky to appear. Footsteps ran back and forth; my heart froze each time they thudded past. The smell of gas-leaking bombs went through my nostrils and the sound of guns pierced through my ears. I put my head down. When was this violent abuse gonna end?

Gabrielle Plant (11)
Eaton Primary School, Tarporley

Human Vs Mummy

500 years ago, it was humans vs mummies. The humans went to an underwater train but the mummies weren't ready for battle. It was midday and Tutankhamun was outside. Tutankhamun had a vision of the humans coming. He shouted, 'The humans are coming, get ready for battle.' They were there and the mummy guards were ready. It started with a *bang! Bang! Bang!* At the end, there were two mummies and one human. They both looked at the ground. The three people made friends and all of them had tea. That was nice.

Henry Roman Copelin (8)
Eaton Primary School, Tarporley

World War I Front Line

France, 1914. I came to fight for what I believe is right, I was told I fought for nations and I fought for my home (Britain). I stood for many days waiting for my time to go into no-man's-land. I knew once I went up, I would die. All night long I heard gunshots, screaming, people falling to the ground. Then it was my turn. I felt a shiver climb my spine. Life flashed before my bleeding eyes and then I went over the top with my courage and for what I thought was right. My heart pounded. *Bang…*

Max O'Shea (10)
Eaton Primary School, Tarporley

World At War

Dear Diary, today we invaded the Germans' military base. We all lined up, shots were fired, grenades were thrown. The acrid smoke filled my lungs. I watched my fellow men fall at my feet. The gunshots blistered my ears; it made my hands tremble. Fighter jets roared over my head, I knew I needed to get out of there. I took cover behind a toppled lorry - everything went silent. I crawled under a car, oil dripped down my face. The German soldiers marched up and down. A young boy looked at me...

Sam Heaton (11)
Eaton Primary School, Tarporley

Troy

My ship pulled up on the Trojan beach, pools of blood oozed into the sea. Screams of dying soldiers filled the air, death felt close. When night had passed, battle had already begun. I grabbed my sword and ran outside, knowing that it would take one shot from an archer to kill me. *Bang!* An arrow bounced off my shield. *Bang! Bang!* Again I was getting shot at much more powerfully. I was sprinting at the wall then an arrow hit my leg. Death was inevitable. I had to think, and fast…

Will Robinson (11)
Eaton Primary School, Tarporley

The Mummy

He strikes again! The long, wild vine crumbles to the muddy, hard ground. Then he saw a huge, outstanding pyramid. With his large, mighty axe he bravely chopped down the opening entrance. Totally overwhelmed, his knees were covered by a lot of valuable gold. The man greedily took all of the gold. He heard a growling sound, he said, 'Hello?' But nobody answered… He turned on his torch and there was a smelly old mummy! As quick as a flash, the man ran away…

Gabriel Quin D'Carroll (8)
Eaton Primary School, Tarporley

The Mummy Curse

It was Thursday, a miserable day, downstairs Dad was making a time machine so I whizzed down the stairs to see what was happening. I was standing behind the door when Dad opened it and marched into the kitchen, I sneaked into the room with the time machine, tried it out, and *whoosh!* I was in ancient Egypt stood right next to a pyramid. I walked through the pyramid in fear, I started to pick up some treasure but then the mummy woke and lifted the coffin lid up…

Sophie Newton (9)
Eaton Primary School, Tarporley

The Battle Commences!

I paced back and forth, frantically wondering when it would happen. Then it finally did… King Richard ran inside the castle. I dashed out of the turret onto the battlefield with my bow, taking down every possible soldier, trying to defend Richard from all of Prince John's soldiers, but when I looked up at the left turret, Richard was there and an arrow was flying towards him… so, with my bow, I pointed it at the arrow and fired, and yet again I was a hero.

Louis Pointon (11)
Eaton Primary School, Tarporley

Theseus And The Minotaur

The seas were rough, Crete was in sight. I could picture the Minotaur roaring, slaying all of the other innocent people. The thought passed my mind as we arrived in Crete. The evil king was standing there with a smug grin on his face, I knew what I had to do, I had to kill the Minotaur. I ventured in the maze, clutching a piece of string. I had my sword, I was ready to take on the Minotaur. I heard screams and roaring, but I went on, not knowing what could happen…

Sean Bowkett (10)
Eaton Primary School, Tarporley

Untitled

After the Christmas Day football match, the gross warfare continued. Bagpipes blew, we all charged and shot each other with guns. My friend was shooting at me, I hid in a hole cremated by mortar fire. Then I shot four Germans trying to throw grenades in my crater I was hiding in. I made a push up to a bunker that was cleared out by the British. My German friend and I stepped out of the trench, we both fired. I survived, my friend James Muller did not.

Jack Robinson (11)
Eaton Primary School, Tarporley

Trial By Fire

'You, Cyrus the Second, King of Florence, have committed an outrageous war crime,' Eriketheous bellowed. 'I hereby condemn you to death!'
'Lord Jupiter,' Hera moaned, 'our noble son has been murdered by Eriketheous.'
'He and his wretched city shall face my rage!' Jupiter shouted mournfully. 'Vulcan, Helios hear my cry, rid Earth of Eriketheous and his people.'
The two gods heard their king's coherent cry. 'Their legendary volcano shall be their doom.'
Vulcan smiled in vengeance. 'My son, Noacous, evacuate Pompeii.' Nocous did so instantly and cowardly.
The next morning, Pompeii was in ruins. No one rebuilt the city.

Kamyar Marashi (11)
Middlemarch School, Nuneaton

Satan's Story

If you don't know the story of Zeus you don't know about his brother, Hades. Zeus is a god amongst men, but Hades is a pure devil - he stops in the Underworld.

One day, Hades had a son. Hades' wife died in childbirth. His son was called Satan, and this is Satan's story.

Zeus went to visit Satan almost every week. Zeus saw that Satan was not happy being an evil person - he wanted to be good; a god amongst men. Then his dad said, 'You will die… ' He killed Satan, just because he wasn't evil, like him.

Leigha Cooper (11)
Middlemarch School, Nuneaton

Red Void

In the year 2016, the unthinkable happened. From that moment on, everything changed. Annie Ackerman, an 11-year-old girl, poverty-stricken and wielding a broken arm, caused this drastic change. She had inadvertently fallen into the year 1000 BC, and was trapped in the world of the Egyptians. Prosperity was not something Annie was familiar with but, even so, the first night she spent in the desert was the worst night of her life.

That morning, when she woke, she ate a lamentable breakfast of the bread she had in her bag, then waited until the ruby void engulfed her once again…

Georgia Beck (11)
Middlemarch School, Nuneaton

A Heist Gone Wrong

Bewildered in my work, I had stupidly not anticipated the night guard patrolling the bank, creeping up to my friend who was busy hacking into the safe. Just when the guard was about to turn the corner, radiant beams of the gold-yellow shone down from the Empyrean Medallion in the now-turning-light-blue sky. He turned around, the sun signalling the end of his shift. The safe door opened with a whoosh, as the air escaped. 'You're in, stuff the bag.'

'Roger that.' My ears addressed footsteps behind me. I looked behind. A cloaked man with a gun appeared…

Durlav Katwal (11)
Middlemarch School, Nuneaton

Egyptian Shadow

Hoo! Hoo! The midnight owl's call woke an 18-year-old. Loka rubbed her eyes. Out of her mud hut window, she looked. She saw the black shadow nightmare spell out a sentence in glittering sparkles: 'Give up your life or I'll take your countries'. Then the pyramid's bricks formed numbers. '1.00, 59… ' Loka leapt out of bed and ran for the door. '50, 49… ' She ran out of the clay house and across the cold, dark desert. '30, 29… ' She tripped over a stone. '20, 19… ' She stopped outside the pyramid. Should she? Yes. She stepped into Death, into the unknown…

Nyah Phoenix (11)
Middlemarch School, Nuneaton

Malek's Vengence

The people were restless. It was several thousand years BC and a vengeful spirit, Malek, had returned after his long dormancy. The people had done him wrong by banishing him from the realm, he would destroy them. Another deity, Cheron, descended from the skies to combat Malek. Bright flashes of blue and black ricocheted across the village. As they hit certain spots, they exposed the invisible forms of Malek and Cheron. As Malek advanced towards Cheron, he corrupted or destroyed everything. Cheron charged an unbelievably powerful attack. He was vulnerable. The beam fired, striking Malek, destroying him on the spot.

Adam Ehsan (10)
Middlemarch School, Nuneaton

The Everyday Life Of Cosmic-Guy

The bioluminescent sun rose up from the ground. Cosmic-Guy woke from his laziness. 'Time to kill,' Cosmic-Guy said. Cosmic-Guy rose from his bed. He raised his hand, lava appeared from his volcano lair. It wreaked havoc on the townspeople. A random guy appeared from a house. *Boom!* The ground rumbled. Trees shook. Cosmic-Guy sent a black-hole dart into the random guy's back. He was sent into a deadly void of blackness. Horror. Death. A random Roman appeared. The sky turned red. A meteor appeared from the sky. Falling, rocketing to the ground. The meteor landed, the world was destroyed.

Samuel Hockley (11)
Middlemarch School, Nuneaton

The End Of Zeus

Zeus sat on a cloud as he tried to gain more power by using his wooden, decrepit wand. He suddenly looked down, his powers had stopped working; he began to fall to the void of Earth. Halfway down he saw his brother. Zeus' heart froze. *What was he doing here?* he asked himself. His brother froze, glaring at him with his piercing black eyes. That's when his brother reached out his hand, gripping onto Zeus' wooden stick. They began to fight. Then suddenly Zeus realised his heart had started bleeding. Zeus was overpowered by his brother.

Poppy Jones (10)
Middlemarch School, Nuneaton

The Freed Prisoners

Luke woke up, remembering everything. He was captured; he was put in a concentration camp. Next to him, Luke saw a rifle. Struggling to move a muscle, Luke stood up - rifle in hand. Suddenly, he remembered his grenade and threw it at the iron door. *Boom!* The door exploded. He crouched and peeked out, spotting crowds of German enemies. He leaped out and shot them to the rhythm of the rattle of the gun. Bodies splatted to the ground. Finding the key, Luke opened the barbed metal door. The freed prisoners ran. Luke could return to his own unit.

Corey Yuile (11)
Middlemarch School, Nuneaton

Ancient Aliens

Long ago, there was a hot and tiring place, which is still here, ancient Egypt. There lived ancient aliens, who wanted to invade countries, but one day Blob said, 'We don't know where to start invading Your Majesty.' So, the nasty and ugly king told them to start invading from Viking Land all the way to Greece Land. They all started sailing from Egypt, it took them six months to sail. When they reached there, they started burning houses and got caught, so they all had to run back. Then the king killed them all. Also, the king died.

Eiman Zahid (10)
Middlemarch School, Nuneaton

The Alien Invasion

Hi, my name is Olivia, I am an 11-year-old girl who is trying to stop beasts causing a battle. The wind howled, loose pebbles tumbled to the ground and stones trickled down my coat. Hope was their only victim - life was their enemy. My heart froze; my jaw dropped. The aliens belted for the exit while the beast choked them with his horrible fire launching out of his endless mouth. The beast licked his lips - not even touching the roof of his mouth. A growl came out of nowhere. Horror was my enemy. Horror! The wind whistled…

Olivia Rhodes (11)
Middlemarch School, Nuneaton

The Discovery

Wandering the Earth's creation, Zac and Karl found a secret cave. A mummy was on a table abandoned for year. Karl unwrapped it, the eyebrows raised! They hadn't seen anything like this before. The mummy leaned up and opened his eyes. A flash! 'Run!' screamed Karl. They ran into a dead end, they thought, *we're so dead.* The mummy got dissected by Zac's dad. They thought they'd killed it…

Leo Drew (11)
Middlemarch School, Nuneaton

The Galaxy Globe

'Armstrong, it's time to go and you'd better hurry,' commanded Buzz.

'I'm coming!' replied Armstrong.

They zoomed and then they went. *Boom!*

Suddenly, Buzz screeched, 'Neil, where are we?'

'I don't know, I'm not sure if we are stuck in the middle of the galaxy. I could try to re-... '

'Don't try, do it!'

'Buzz, look! Something's going to... ' *Boom!* 'Buzz, are you alive?' mumbled Neil.

'Are you?'

'Should we go home?'

'Yeah, let's do that.'

Taya Edwards-Sowomi (10)
St John The Baptist Primary School, London

The Eagle Has Landed

The background was full of midnight-black. The ground was like powdered charcoal. The only thing I could see was the humongous, creamy surface of the moon. 'Houston, Tranquillity Base here. The Eagle has landed.' I mumbled.

'You should probably take some samples,' Buzz shouted.

'Nice idea, but don't shout at me, Buzz,' I replied.

I took some samples and heard a dreadful noise but I was still ecstatic. I turned around, my heart froze. 'What's that?' I shouted.

'It looks like a meteor!' Buzz yelled.

We knew something horrendous would happen. There was nowhere to go.

Darren Osei Sarfo (10)
St John The Baptist Primary School, London

The Star And Striped Flag Is Planted

The ground was rock hard and the background was jet-black. I stepped on the moon and it felt like being the first ever president. The floor was powdered charcoal. You couldn't see anything but planets. 'Houston, Tranquillity Base here. The Eagle has landed,' I boasted.

Buzz answered, 'If you want people to know, you'd better have some samples!'

I shouted back happily, 'I will have some samples, I will have lots of them!'

We were bounding around the moon, when our oxygen started to run out. We were ready to leave and we noticed it was at five percent...

Jason O'Connor (10)
St John The Baptist Primary School, London

Breakdown On The Moon

Everything was platinum and charcoal. Neil Armstrong floated off the Millennium Falcon 7000, the fast starship and anxious Buzz was impatient. They were surrounded by midnight stars shining through space. 'Do I have to wait forever, Captain Neil?' Neil Armstrong saw a star zooming like a racing car, called a Bugatti. After a star, a ruby blossom line appeared... He thought it was a meteor but it was something that was bigger! As Buzz Aldrin turned around, he saw it was a humongous monster ship. It had a crimson light. 'Help! Help!'
'Get Neil!'
Roar!

Royal Edorh (10)
St John The Baptist Primary School, London

Houston Arrives On The Moon

The stars had arrived on the plain white moon. The moon was as white as snow. I arrived with my partner, Buzz, in the endless space full of stars.
'Look Buzz, there's a rock heading our way. It would wreck our ship.'
'Well I... I think it's probably a hologram.'
We went in the spacecraft made by NASA. As I was in the ship, I stared. A headache arrived, I was sweating the closer the rock came.
'Wow, it's pretty c-close.' It left a trail of ash behind. *Boom!*

Daniel Aduqbole (10)
St John The Baptist Primary School, London

One Step On The Moon

Neil Armstrong could hear his heart beating as he stepped onto the moon softly. Buzz Aldrin was repairing the ship and trying to start it. It was pitch-black except for the stars that were shining over the moon. 'Houston, Tranquillity Base here. The Eagle has landed,' Neil Armstrong stated, overjoyed.
'I will be back with you shortly,' Buzz remarked.
'That is one small step for man, one giant leap for mankind.' Armstrong went to collect samples then he suddenly disappeared in the powdery dust...
Buzz Aldrin tried to get a signal, but nothing was there...

Grace Cole (10)
St John The Baptist Primary School, London

The Eagle Has Arrived

Once upon a time on a day in 1969, a team of astronauts did the unthinkable. At exactly 2:36 GMT, the Eagle landed for the first time. The midnight sky greeted them, when they arrived. At approximately 2.56 GMT, triumphant Armstrong stepped on the chalky surface and became the first to set foot upon the moon. 'Collect some samples before mission abort!'
shouted astronaut, Buzz Aldrin.
Suddenly, luminous lights touched down, green men took Armstrong. 'Help me, Buzz... Buzz!'

Aalenya Reece (10)
St John The Baptist Primary School, London

He Was Searching For Me, Only Me!

I woke up, a normal day, or was it?
Coming out from the shadows of my home,
nervously thinking about the dragon who controls
the village, every hour, every day. I knew I had to
change the fear. He cannot rule us forever! I was
confident, ready for battle.
I bit my tongue, clenched my fists. I
slithered silently down from my cave. Trees
cowered. The sun looked away from the village. I
would save my town!
I charged towards the colossal dragon, daring to
blink, he blew fire at me, but missed! I slayed him!
Victory was ours.

Cecile Reeves (10)
St Paul's CE Primary School, London

The Girl Who Wanted To See The Minotaur

There was a girl called Sofy, she wanted to see the Minotaur. Well, the king said, 'No!' Sofy didn't listen, she got ready for the journey. Those kind of creatures live in forests.

A day later, Sofy was just in front of the cave. She took ten steps. Looking back then forward, Sofy saw the Minotaur. He pushed her stomach with his bright horns. Sofy just realised she didn't have any weapons so she wasn't really ready for the journey! The Minotaur roared, she was speechless. The Minotaur showed her its teeth, there was nothing Soft could do.

'Argh!'

Fope Haroun (9)
St Paul's CE Primary School, London

Diana's Life

There was once a lovely girl called Diana. She worked in a market to get money. She lived in a poor house next to dirt and dust, it was dreadful. One day, she went to pray at the beautiful temple. She prayed to get rich.

The next day, when Diana was waking up and waking her children, she saw she'd become rich. Their house was made out of beautiful gold and there were waiters. Diana loved it so much that nearly fainted. But one day she saw some people working in the market and she decided to work there.

Lyra Butcher (9)
St Paul's CE Primary School, London

The Helpless Gladiator

The gladiator was slumped on a rock, eyes closed, dreaming. The cave leaked with blood. Suddenly, the iron bars opened with a thunderous crash. Daylight shimmered as Leous the gladiator's eyes squeezed. Leous walked out, he grabbed a sword and shield. A cacophony of noise spread around the Colosseum. It was a lion. The lion scratched Leous' eye, he fell down and immediately was pounced on. The crowd roared with laughter. Leous had to be taken in.

Hours later, Leous returned to the ring, sword in hand, ready to fight, blood drooling down him. Leous charged at the lion...

Leon Francis White (9)
St Paul's CE Primary School, London

Beast

The antidote was wrong. I'm Beast. Me and my dragon will defeat Monstrous.

We were face-to-face. It had red eyes, sharp claws, black scales. My claws sprouted. Its claws sprouted. *Cling, clang, clong.* Our claws met. Greek warriors screamed below. My claws sank into its chest. The scream it made was the loudest I'd ever heard. As soon as it started bleeding, it grew back again. I took out my chain and threw it on Monstrous. Suddenly, my form was human again. I knew I wouldn't be able to defeat Monstrous like this so I ran very far...

Ariel Leeb (9)
St Paul's CE Primary School, London

Cerceuce And King Cumbra

On one sunny day in ancient Greece, there was a small house. In the house lived a young, brave and strong boy called Cerceuce. He lived with his mother called Lovely. His dad was killed by the king.

One day, he thought that maybe he should kill the king. So he smacked into the beautiful palace and saw the king. He ran for his life and shouted, 'You are evil!' He stopped running and took a knife out of his pocket and stabbed the king in the heart. The king's knees were trembling as he fell to the floor dead...

Lucy-Lou Collis (9)
St Paul's CE Primary School, London

The Deadly Change

I suddenly woke up. I felt different. I looked at myself in a mirror, I had a tail, wings, claws and jagged teeth. I smelt blood, it smelt good. I opened the door, now the smell was stronger. I bit a man, digging my teeth into his arm and a lovely taste flooded into my mouth.

Years passed, I killed many people. One day, Hades met me, he said he wanted to punish the souls who had been threatening his wife. I agreed. Now I work for Hades, he has given me many thousands of tasks. I've never failed.

Luke Naumovic (9)
St Paul's CE Primary School, London

The Chimera's Last Dinner

It was a nice day and I was lying in bed till my mum came and said I was to be called up to the King of Naxos. She looked pale. When I was there he told me what had happened. Now I knew why she was pale.

I was at the Chimera's lair. Trembling and biting my tongue, I stepped forward. There were yellow eyes in the dark and grumbling sounds. Suddenly, Perseus came. He took his sword out and swung it. On the way home, I fell asleep. I woke up and found out Perseus had betrayed me.

Aisha Abdulaziz (9)
St Paul's CE Primary School, London

The Rise Of The Monsters

I sprint down the gravel path in the forest. 'Argh!' I've sprained my ankle but that's not the worst, it's a scout party of monsters coming my way. The trees cower as their jagged, razor claws come into view. I need help, now! I crawl to my village but I can't see anyone. The monsters are the least of my worries. Nope. *Still they're the biggest*, I think, as the Chimera appears. I throw my dagger. Suddenly, there's an ear-piercing scream. The Chimera lets out a last breath, then falls to the ground dead, other monsters are after me...

Harvey Nightingale (9)
St Paul's CE Primary School, London

The Beast!

As the trees dance and the sun looks down onto Earth, I stroll along the path. Suddenly there's a rustling in a bush nearby, and a creature jumps out. It has red, round eyes and razor-sharp claws. I immediately start running as fast as my legs will carry me. *Don't. Look. Back.* I see a crowd all around me, cheering which makes me run faster. A man stops me. He says, 'You have won the Olympics!' I try to run out of his grasp but it is tight. I look over my shoulder. The beast is gone. For now...

Amelia Pike (9)
St Paul's CE Primary School, London

The Unknown Island

I waited endlessly. Nothing, no sign of land.
I'd been sailing for days, our food supply was low
and, what was this... oh Lord! There was land.
'Forward men. We're on land.' But I was wrong,
there was a... monster! 'Run for your lives!' I said.
Clutching my fists and biting my lip, I sprinted faster
than I ever had. Then I looked back and there it
stood on four legs. I stared at his furry arms and
legs in horror, I knew this time there was no escape
at all. I watched my men die and that was it.

Aylan Touat (9)
St Paul's CE Primary School, London

The Lost Man

I'm finding it hard to breathe, I'm feeling dizzy. I'm lost, I'm being hunted. I see a city in the distance, I stop. I'm being hunted, I have to keep running. I look around. There is nothing. I start running again. 'Faster, faster,' I tell myself. I've reached the city. I turn around, the dragon glides at top speed. He spits his poison at me, I just dodge it. I run over all the smashed bricks. I jump over a smashed sculpture then the poison hits me. After that I scare him off for now.

Max Scantlebury (9)
St Paul's CE Primary School, London

Odysseus And The Cyclops

One day, when war had ended, on a ship, a hero called Odysseus was on his way home until... Odysseus started to throw rubbish in the sea. Poseidon was so mad he destroyed the ship but luckily they landed in a cave, It had lots of dairy products. They started eating until a big voice said, 'Who dares to eat my food?' It was a Cyclops. Odysseus got his sword and then the Cyclops was blinded but an eye grew back and so Odysseus got his arrow and shot him in the heart! The monster was dead, war was over.

Saira Ali (9)
St Paul's CE Primary School, London

The Greek Attack

I felt fearless walking slowly. I was waiting till my dad came back. Suddenly, I saw a ship, it felt like I'd waited ages. Oh no, it was the enemy's ship. It came faster than ever. Swords piercing, I picked up my seeds and ran again. Then I was in pure fear, a strong man was chasing me. He tried to stab me but I ducked and jumped in the water. Then *slash!* I was floating down, I was drowning. Then my last views were smashed... I floated away and I was forgotten forever. It was the end of life.

Felix Pinyol (9)
St Paul's CE Primary School, London

The Chimera

The grass waved silently, the trees danced and I sprinted up the path. But something made me stop. There was a deafening roar, a horrible hiss, and an angry stamp. I gave an everlasting scream, as the Chimera emerged out of the trees. The moment it saw me, it charged and I ran for dear life. Suddenly, I turned around and there it was, right in front of me. Its beady yellow eyes stared into mine. I was about to run again, but all went black. I landed in a little village. The Chimera was gone, for now...

Anine Christinsen (9)
St Paul's CE Primary School, London

The Magical Creature

I run and run and run. My heart beats rapidly. I don't know how I ended up here and I don't know why there are strange creatures all around me. I don't even know how I'm going to get back! I ignore what my conscience is telling me and look back. Horrified, I scream. The creatures around me run away in fear as the sand shoots up into the air. The sun reaches out and touches my eyes as I look back at the creature's beady, black eyes and scaly skin and - wait! A river...

Martha Reynolds (9)
St Paul's CE Primary School, London

The Bottomless Pit

It ran right at me. *Uff!* I fell. I woke up and saw a dragon fly by me and whack me with its tail, but I kept falling. I heard a deafening hiss, it was the Hydra. I saw a red thing in mid-air, a wriggly, squirming thing. Then it disappeared. The Hydra flew across. It cut my knee, I guessed this was the Hydra's lair. I saw a pit of snakes. They were bush vipers. Was this the sweet, sweet release of death? The Hydra hissed, I was ready to fight its ferocious claws...

Dario Velazquez (9)
St Paul's CE Primary School, London

Being Chased

I was walking in the woods until I heard a roar. Suddenly, something jumped out of the trees. It seemed strange because it had a lion's body, a goat's head and snake's tail. It had round, yellow eyes and they were staring at me. I ran for my life but he was running after me. I sprinted as fast as I could but the monster was faster. Suddenly, I fell down. The monster approached me, I was done for. Then he let out another roar. I was caught...

Aadam Muhammad (9)
St Paul's CE Primary School, London

The God Of The Sea

I was on the beach because I was tired and waiting for my friend, Icy. Icy finally arrived and the trees were blowing but suddenly I heard a deafening scream in front of me. It was Poseidon! I ran but Poseidon was going down and it was very weird, there was nothing to do. The water was dragging me down suddenly he was let go. Icy was back. I heard a big bang and the next thing I knew I was back in my lovely bedroom. But was I safe... ?

Alice Warden (9)
St Paul's CE Primary School, London

Anne Gets The Chop

In the vast Windsor Castle, Anne and Henry were having a delightful conversation about who killed who. Henry apparently had slashed the French in a so-called 'battle'; whereas Anne had defeated the Scots, their mortal enemy, while Henry had only killed ten soldiers. Then Henry boomed at Anne, 'While I was away at France during my battle you defeated the Scots! I, Henry VIII sentence you, Anne Boleyn to death!'
'Henry, please! Don't... Noooo!'
The next day, Anne wearily placed her head on the the block and then... *splat!* Anne's head tumbled on the floor and Henry regretted his decision.

Júlia Viguier Souto (9)
St Peter's Catholic Primary School, Leamington Spa

The Killing Of The Evil Spirit

Readers beware, you're in for a scare! Muhanzee and his uncle were nowhere to be seen, and that was because he was in Egypt. The place where people go missing: the Pyramid of Giza! Surprisingly, peasants believed that an evil spirit haunted the pyramid, but that was only in his home country. Muhanzee and his uncle wanted to win that glorious cash prize and become rich. They needed to find that mummified pharaoh. As they quickly rumbled across the door, *boom!* The door slammed shut. 'That scared the life out of me!' said Muhanzee.

'Mwahaha!'

'Uh-oh!'

Luke Cashman (8)
St Peter's Catholic Primary School, Leamington Spa

The Mummy Finds His Pharaoh

Sand trickled down the never-ending walls, blood splattered on the ground. Without warning, a petrifying white monster stumbled round the corner, his arms outstretched like a ruthless zombie. The mummy screamed, longing for a fresh body to devour. Suddenly, a cry echoed off the walls, the guards were coming... The mummy stretched his legs and, groaning madly, went into a full run. The tomb walls zoomed past, his bandages just a blur. All of a sudden, the mummy skidded to a halt, a golden cot in front of him, a man inside. 'Come to Mummy!'
'No!' he screamed... dead...

James Foley (10)
St Peter's Catholic Primary School, Leamington Spa

The Dinosaurs Are Still Alive

It was a boiling day. The dinosaurs were munching on grass, but deep down in the Earth, magma churned and bubbled. Out in space a meteor was speeding towards Earth at an alarming rate. Suddenly, back on Earth, trees started falling, the ground was shaking: it was an earthquake.
Two weeks later, the earthquake was about to catapult the dinosaurs into space. Seconds later, the massive meteor hit the Earth at the fastest speed known to man. The Earth burst into a fireball. Everything was destroyed. But in a galaxy far away the dinosaurs were still alive...

Thomas Connell (9)
St Peter's Catholic Primary School, Leamington Spa

The War Machine

I grabbed my shiny gun, I looked up, the enemy soldiers were stamping forward. Suddenly, a man with a bleeding leg appeared in sight, he was a scout. 'We've got to get out of here! The weapon, they have the-... Argh!' He fell to the ground. George looked at me.
'No way James, we're going to die, we never thought it was ready.' *Boom!* The front of our bunker exploded. I held my gun and fired. A shiny nozzle appeared out of the darkness. Then a colossal metallic body crept forwards. It was a tank, it was the British Mark!

Daniel Bodely (9)
St Peter's Catholic Primary School, Leamington Spa

The Labyrinth

The ground was rumbling with fear. I was in a labyrinth. Running, I saw a Minotaur as big as a house. 'Raaar!' roared the Minotaur. I gasped. The Minotaur got closer and closer. My shivering hand reached for my sword. I flung my sword at the Minotaur, missed and the Minotaur charged at me. I drove myself out of the way. As quick as a flash, I rushed to the exit, but it followed me. 'Roar!' roared the Minotaur.
'Argh!' I screamed. I kept running. Suddenly, I tripped over a rock. 'Argh!' Closer and closer it got...

Ben Foley (8)
St Peter's Catholic Primary School, Leamington Spa

The Historical World War

The field floor was rumbling as the rotten Romans were charging towards the Royal English army. There was a big storm like elephants barging across trees. 'Argh!' Two teams were yelling as they barged into each other. As they bashed into each other, you could hear the tinging as the shiny metal shields bashed together. *Ting!* It echoed. *Neigh!* the armoured horses cried. The Romans would stand their ground but by surprise the queen's husband knocked the rotten Roman emperor off his horse. Just then, the rotten Romans surrendered. 'Hooray!' Britain shouted. The Royal family won!

Zach Miah (8)
St Peter's Catholic Primary School, Leamington Spa

The Transformation

In Victorian times it was dusty. An inventor, called Mr Bookington, made a brilliant machine called The Love-o-Meter. It was good of him to make this amazing machine because it would make the world a better place. He used it and made that street colourful and kinder. Suddenly, he heard someone shouting at him, it was the Queen. She told him to stop doing it because the world would be frightening. She shouted, 'You'll be in prison if you do it again!' Mr Bookington, up to mischief, was sent to jail. He escaped then secretly used his fantastic, amazing machine.

Maisie Young (9)
St Peter's Catholic Primary School, Leamington Spa

The Mummy's Coming!

Regularly, Lucy would be sleeping. Nevertheless, today she was taking a petrifying walk into Tutankhamun's tomb. Lucy was a powerful girl; she always focused on things. Suddenly, a mummy vaulted out of nowhere. Never in Lucy's life had she seen a mummy. The mummy hunted her; finally it got her. Lucy was very frightened. When the mummy had got Lucy it started to mumble this, 'I'm Tutankhamun and I'm coming for everyone in Egypt for mummifying me!' Lucy was terrified. When the mummy caught her he wrapped her up and put her in his tomb.

Ropa Kazora (8)
St Peter's Catholic Primary School, Leamington Spa

C-R-E-E-P-E-R Spells Trouble

The Roman had finished making his pixel gun. Surprisingly, a magic room appeared! It was a time machine. A suspicious, green creature stepped out. The Roman pulled the trigger. The ray swerved past the creeper, who had no arms. Then he ran inside a telephone box. He called Steve. Steve brought his bright, shiny diamond sword. The Roman pulled the trigger on the pixel gun. It shot Steve! He disappeared. In the blink of an eye, the Roman pulled the trigger again. It bounced off a light and zapped the Roman! The creeper grabbed the gun. Oh no! Not again!

Oli Passantino (8)
St Peter's Catholic Primary School, Leamington Spa

The Victorious Vikings

The Vikings swooshed their dark, pitch-black axes at the vicious-looking Anglo-Saxons, as they charged towards them. Vikings, Eric and James, charged as fast as they could in their buffalo fur armour with their golden bracelets. Eric and James were all of a sudden outnumbered and against 60,000 men. They had to surrender, they had to, but Eric and James weren't quitters, so they did fight and they did not give up. They were victorious, the Vikings had won, they had beaten the mighty Anglo-Saxons. Now there was one left, but they could beat him.

Sebastian Bainbridge (9)
St Peter's Catholic Primary School, Leamington Spa

The Boy And The Sabre-Toothed Tiger

Trembling, the boy slowly walked into the deep, dark cave filled with beautiful cave paintings. In the corner of the cave, the boy noticed a massive pile of rocks. As the boy walked on, the rocks began to rumble. The boy stopped, loose rocks began to fall from the roof and then... *roar!* As quick as lightning, a fearsome creature jumped out of the pile of rocks. It was a sabre-toothed tiger. The boy lay down as still as a statue and stroked the sabre-toothed tiger's face, and climbed on his back. The two became best hunters together.

Jack Dando (9)
St Peter's Catholic Primary School, Leamington Spa

The Grave Robbers

A girl and her crew went to Egypt. They met Cleopatra, she gave them a tour. Behind Cleopatra's back the grave robbers stole things. Anubis warned the Captain, 'Don't steal a thing.' But she didn't listen. She stole more things. Cleopatra talked to Anubis and Anubis couldn't help it and killed the grave robbers! Cleopatra shouted, 'There's one more.' Then Anubis spread an evil smile across his face! He zoomed with his mummies and he found her, she tried to run, she was horrified. She got killed by Anubis.

Loretta Memetovic (9)
St Peter's Catholic Primary School, Leamington Spa

The Horrifying Wolf!

It was the middle of the night, the moon was full, but something was wrong. From the distance came a long, terrifying howl. It was coming closer and closer. The floor was rumbling as if there was thunder. Everybody sleeping in the palace had had horrible nightmares. The queen froze! But before she could say a word, something bit her and carried her away. When she woke up, she found herself in Rome. She was so petrified that she screamed as if the crown was stolen. In a while, she heard something but instead of people, she saw a wolf...

Wiki Jakubczyk (8)
St Peter's Catholic Primary School, Leamington Spa

Egyptians Vs Vikings

One horrible century, the Egyptians were full of anger at the Vikings. The Egyptians reached their swords ready to have revenge on the Vikings. The gods went at the front. The battle was close, the Egyptian souls were trying to take the Vikings' souls. The weak nearly died but were strong, so they didn't die. They were full of blood. Some gods were alive, others weren't. They slashed each other with their owners. The Egyptians growled at the Vikings like tigers trying to rip someone's arms off with anger!

Guilherme Berlino Pinto (8)

St Peter's Catholic Primary School, Leamington Spa

Death Run

I stared at the creaky old floor. The damp, wet floor had traces of blood from the monster I faced a year ago. It had returned. More powerful than ever before. All of a sudden, a ferocious roar came from the depths of the cave. *He's coming*, I thought to myself. The wind whistled in my ears. I froze from the shock of the monster. It stared at me with its blood-red eyes. It came closer. Its razor-sharp claws pierced my skin. I drew my sword and stabbed it through the leg. It was weak, it died!

Samuel Divers (8)
St Peter's Catholic Primary School, Leamington Spa

Clumsy Cavemen

The wind howled and the moon shone as bright as silver. I was in a deep sleep, even though the floor was rock hard. It was very uncomfortable. I was sleeping on a hard, round rock. I jerked awake... Large footprints were approaching my cave. I was terrified! There was a thrash on top of me. I peeped outside, there was a humongous dinosaur ruining my house. Soon my cave was half gone. My hands were trembling and there was panic in my body. I got banged on the head. I woke up confused. Was it a nightmare?

Amelia Smith (8)
St Peter's Catholic Primary School, Leamington Spa

The War

John was walking into the distance looking for a river to catch some fish. He strolled off into the open. In the blink of an eye, John was in the range of a German gun. Quickly, he jumped down into a trench. Everything was silent. Then there was a bomb seconds later. John was enveloped by the bomb, everyone was dead, gone, lost forever. John got in one of the vans and went to the nearest village, everyone was dead, wiped out for miles. There was no civilisation. John felt lost, sad, helpless.

James Pearson (9)
St Peter's Catholic Primary School, Leamington Spa

The Mystery Tomb

Sand brushed against my feet, I was standing in the Valley of the Kings. I walked into a tomb, I could not see anything apart from darkness. I felt something grab my leg! It was a trap. I quickly jumped out of the way. I heard a loud voice that echoed down the tomb, I knew I would not be able to go much further, so I went back. I heard the voice again but it was quieter. When I got out I went straight to the van that we came in. They said they would brick up the wall.

Kieran O'Connor (9)
St Peter's Catholic Primary School, Leamington Spa

War With The Caesars

The ground was rumbling. Suddenly, a moment later, six royal horses strode in sturdily. Julius Gaius Caesar then shouted, 'Alas, fair friends, I wish you the compliments of the season!' A person, named Brutus, was ignoring him deliberately. Then, thinking of what Liatus had said, he got back to his villa. Seeing that he had his men in their gleaming armour standing before the sunset, he was ready to strike Julius Caesar...

Valentin Bonnet-Aumann (8)
St Peter's Catholic Primary School, Leamington Spa

I And A Half-Mummy And Half-Human

Myself and my family were in a pyramid, checking out the half-mummy and the half-human! This weird creature was almost fully white but the most important information you need to know is, it was fierce. I ran for my life, my heart was beating faster and faster! The wind flew past me, it made me even more scared. I yelled as loud as I possibly could!

One day, I hope Egypt has no silly, crazy monsters! I hope the pharaohs will give them punishments, I really wish! Otherwise the half-mummy and half-humans will gobble up other people!

Aaron Rye Bumagat (8)
Thomas's Academy, London

The Viking And Mother Nature

Once upon a time there was a Viking sailing the seven seas.

In the middle of the night there was a big bang coming from the sky. The lightning lit up the seas and the rain came pouring down so hard, crashing against the boat! The waves tossed the Viking's boat from side to side. He was so scared. He prayed to Mother Nature to save him from drowning and she did, he smiled and looked up into the sky and said, 'Thank you Mother Nature.' He carried on sailing the seven seas for many, many more amazing years.

Ricco De Beaufort
Thomas's Academy, London

Stoney The Caveman

On a dusty morning, a man called Stoney was hunting for food. He soon found a big, juicy, yummy mammoth and he couldn't take his eyes off her. Stoney carried the mammoth down the steep hill and started slicing its body and eating the meat. Once he was finished he thought of a terrific idea; instead of him leaving the skin, he made clothes out of it. When he was doing it he noticed a wolf but Stoney wasn't scared because he was a caveman and cavemen didn't get scared. Instantly, Stoney struck the wolf with his sharp sword.

Rihanna Andrews (8)
Thomas's Academy, London

The Mummy And The Diamonds

Long ago, there lived a mummy where diamonds fell from the sky. This was a problem as she was poor and was put under a curse to stay indoors. There was also a haunted doll! The mummy was frightened but she soon found out that he was not bad! He wanted to help. He rose up and demanded to speak to Weather. After knocking some sense into Weather, he came back down. The mummy was freed from her curse and nobody was allowed to receive the diamonds until the mummy got the same amount as most people! Everything was great.

Basma Djenadou (8)
Thomas's Academy, London

The Viking Is Coming

Once upon a time there was a Viking called Toby. He went hunting for animals in the deep, deep forest. Eventually, Viking Toby found some yummy pigs to eat. He killed the pigs with his sharp spear and it went straight through its head. Viking Toby brought the massive pig home to share with other Vikings. All of the Vikings thought up a huge plan. Vikings were going to kill the other Vikings, but instead they became friends with the other Vikings. Then they went to hunt for delicious animals.

Lewis Baptiste (8)
Thomas's Academy, London

A Woman With Lots And Lots Of Gold

Once, a woman was on a beach relaxing. Then she saw an amazing treasure box! She looked right and left and she saw nobody there. So the woman stole the amazing box! After that, the amazing box started to speak to her! She wondered why it was speaking to her but she just ran away with it! Then she found a sad and upset village. The woman went into the village and gave a bit of money to the villagers. She went to see the king and said, 'If you marry me, I'll give you this... '

Anum Muktar (8)
Thomas's Academy, London

The Mystery Of The Kidnapper

The trees blew, stones tumbled down the street and then the kidnapper approached. My jaw fell to the ground, there I was, staring into his frightening eyes. He was so hungry he was dribbling from his cheeky grin. Within a second we were face-to-face. I was petrified like I have never been before. I realised that he had a black mask and very sharp nails. I turned my light on and it was a kidnapper...

Kaci Agullo (8)
Thomas's Academy, London

Mummy Escape

I opened the tomb! Then a mummy leapt out and chased me around the pyramid! When I lost him, I saw a bright flash of fire. Then somehow he managed to get out of the pyramid by climbing through the sand. Then I got him back in the tomb by waving glistening gold. At last, I was safe.

Noah Quicksell (8)
Thomas's Academy, London

The Terrifying Night

One terrifying and frightening night, an Egyptian died, it was the pharaoh, the King of Egypt. Some of the Egyptians were turning the pharaoh into a mummy and left him in a tomb, They left the room that they made the mummies in.

When it was the middle of the night, something was happening... the tomb lid flung open then out came the mummy with bandages hanging off! The people who were doing the mummies were surprised, they quickly ran out of the special room and went to tell the pharaoh's son...

Kristian Fisher (9)
Whithorn Primary School, Newton Stewart

In The Beginning Of History...

Atoms were flying everywhere, massive grey smoke clouds circled, flaming meteors travelled in space so fast. Then it came, the big... *bang!* Was it normal for planets to be created? There was life. It developed crystal-blue waves, bushy moss-coloured green trees. But none of this was as spectacular as the developed creature. A fish then monkey, now a human. You could ask a million questions and none of them have a true answer, it's all such a weird mystery if it happened this way. For now who knows, but it was a very big bang indeed!

Ciara Jolly (11)
Whithorn Primary School, Newton Stewart

Rat King Gets Poisoned By Cheese

One day, Rat King was relaxing in bed, suddenly there was a knocking at the door. It was Rat's servant telling him he had a visitor. It was the human. He offered the king some cheese. They got into a long conversation then it was lunch. Rat King went through the rat hole back to Rat Castle for lunch, he grated his cheese for a sandwich and also he was late for a meeting with his fans. While he spoke, his sandwich that he didn't realise the human had put poison in, gave him a reaction, acting quickly. He died!

Lexi Fisher (11)
Whithorn Primary School, Newton Stewart

Vikings' Attack

There was a Viking called Hanga, he had the best day sailing across the sea. He approached the island and chopped off Irised's head. They all hid around the village and did lots of things. They played cards and then they went to attack a man and then they saw Hanga, so they went to go back to their ship and they got on it and set sail across the sea. There was a big storm and the ship sank and all the Vikings died with only one plank of wood left and one little bubble as well...

Ryan Williams (8)
Whithorn Primary School, Newton Stewart

Alexander The Great

One day in ancient Greece, a man called Alexander, was ready to join the army. The next day, he was going to go into battle, but first he needed a sword and sheath and armour, so he went and got his armour. He went off in his chariot and started to give out his orders. When he reached the battlefield, he shot bullets and his bowman shot at the Persians too. Then Alexander sent his other men to knock them over! They fell down. Alex had won the battle and peace was restored in Greece.

Sean Collins (10)
Whithorn Primary School, Newton Stewart

Sports Day

One day, a year ago, when it was sports day, before we went down to the park, we had to get our water bottles and our chairs and then we were off to the park to have sports day. There were lots of races, there was a running race, a sack race, a mile run and an egg and spoon race. I got three seconds and two thirds, but I did not win anything because someone else in my team did and Crugalton came second. We got ice creams, we ate them and lived happily ever after!

Shiloh Boyce (7)
Whithorn Primary School, Newton Stewart

The Vikings Are Coming

As I was sitting on the beach one day, I saw something on the horizon. As it got closer and closer, I could see a silhouette of a ship. Was it the Vikings? My heart started to beat very fast. I could see the shape of the horns on their helmets. I sat quietly watching and waiting, suddenly there was a loud roar from the ship. The Vikings had landed on the shore. The Vikings were heading straight for me. Had they seen me hiding in the bush?

Amy Vance (8)
Whithorn Primary School, Newton Stewart

Years of YoungWriters

YOUNG WRITERS INFORMATION

We hope you have enjoyed reading this book – and that you will continue to in the coming years.

If you're a young writer who enjoys reading and creative writing, or the parent of an enthusiastic poet or story writer, do visit our website www.youngwriters.co.uk. Here you will find free competitions, workshops and games, as well as recommended reads, a poetry glossary and our blog.

If you would like to order further copies of this book, or any of our other titles give us a call or visit **www.youngwriters.co.uk**.

'HE CAME, HE SAW, HE CONKED US'!

Young Writers
Remus House
Coltsfoot Drive
Peterborough
PE2 9BF

(01733) 890066
info@youngwriters.co.uk